撒希往牙医诊所

Sahir Goes to the Dentist

by Chris Petty

MANDARIN & ENGLISH

Hear each page of this talking book narrated in many languages with TalkingPEN!

1. To get started, touch the arrow button below with the TalkingPEN.
2. Touch the English or language button to select your language.
3. Touch the top corner of any page to hear the text narrated.
4. Touch the square button to hear information about listening to more languages and how to use the TalkingPEN with this book.

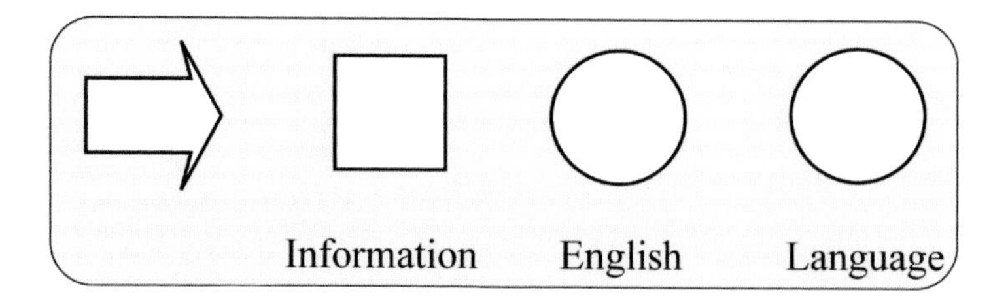

First published in 2006 by Mantra Lingua Ltd
Global House, 303 Ballards Lane
London N12 8NP
www.mantralingua.com

This edition 2014

A CIP record for this book is available from the British Library

撒希往牙医诊所

Sahir Goes to the Dentist

by Chris Petty

Mandarin translation by Sylvia Denham

「爸爸，这牙齿什么时候才掉下来啊？」撒希呻吟著说。
「当它应该掉下时才掉下来，」爸爸答道。
「噢！已经很久了，」撒希叹道。

"Dad, when will this tooth come out?" groaned Sahir.
"When it's ready," replied Dad.
"Aww! It's been ages," sighed Sahir.

他不用等太久，就当他咬进三明治时，他的牙齿便掉下来。
「嘿，爸爸，我现在很像他啊，」撒希骄傲地说。
「至少你会长出一只新牙，」爸爸微笑著说。

He didn't have to wait long. Just as he bit into his sandwich, out came his tooth.
"Hey Dad, I look just like him now," said Sahir proudly.
"Well at least ***you*** will grow a new tooth," said Dad, with a smile.

「我们应该去牙医处检查，确保你的新牙生长妥当，」爸爸说，
他跟着便打电话到牙医处预约时间。

"We should go to the dentist to make sure your new teeth are coming through OK," said Dad and he phoned the dentist for an appointment.

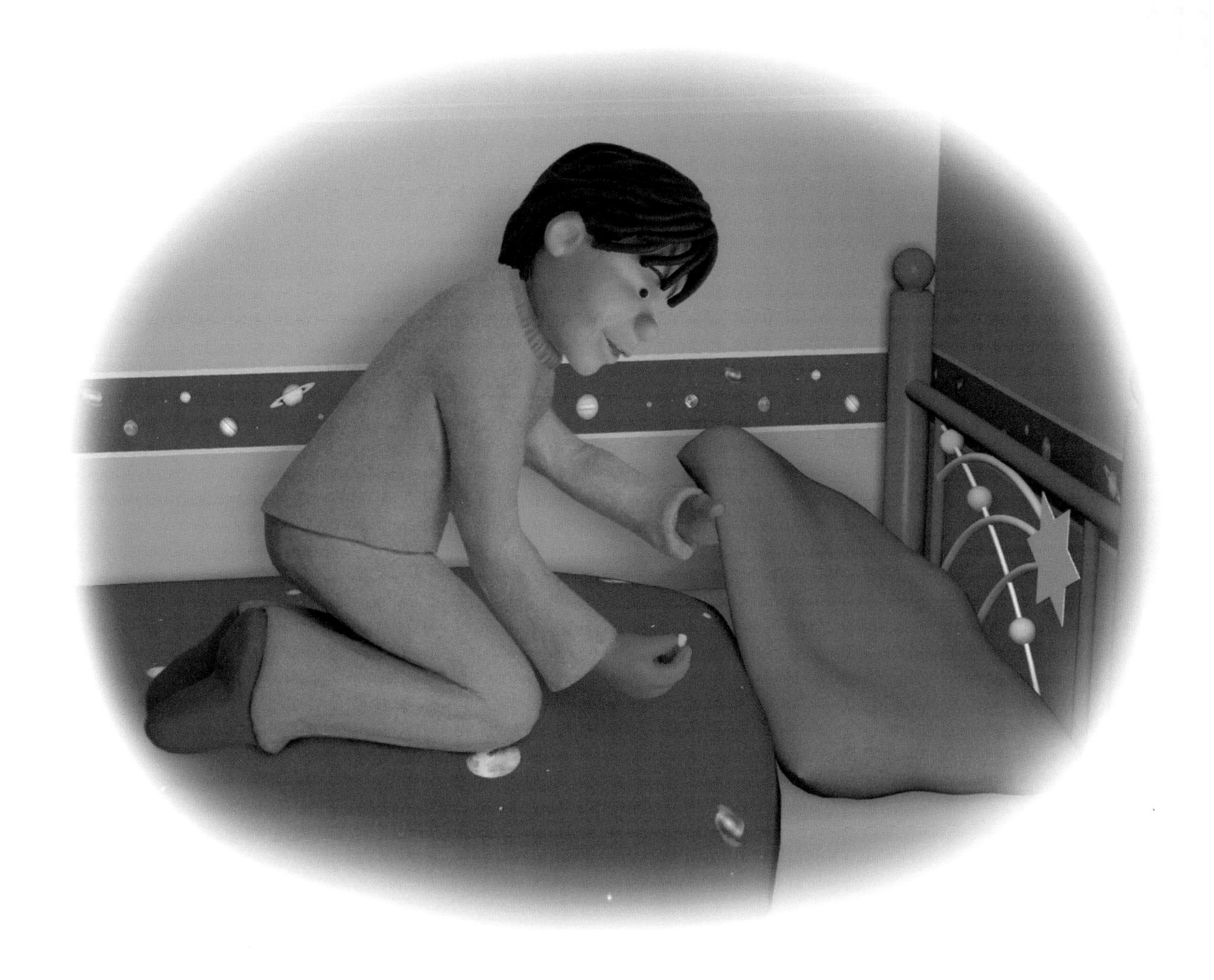

撒希在上床睡觉时把他的牙齿放在枕头下面。

At bedtime Sahir put his tooth under the pillow.

第二天早上，撒希发现一枚钱币。「你看，牙齿仙子来过，」撒希大声叫道。「你可以帮我保管这个吗，爸爸？」

The next morning he found a shiny coin. "Guess what? The tooth fairy came," Sahir shouted. "Can you look after this, Dad?"

「我会买一大块巧克力，」他说。

"I'm going to buy a big bar of chocolate," he said.

第二天，撒希、雅思敏和爸爸一起到牙医诊所处。

The next day Sahir, Yasmin and Dad all went to the dentist.

他们在候诊室坐著等候牙医。

They sat in the waiting-room until the dentist was ready.

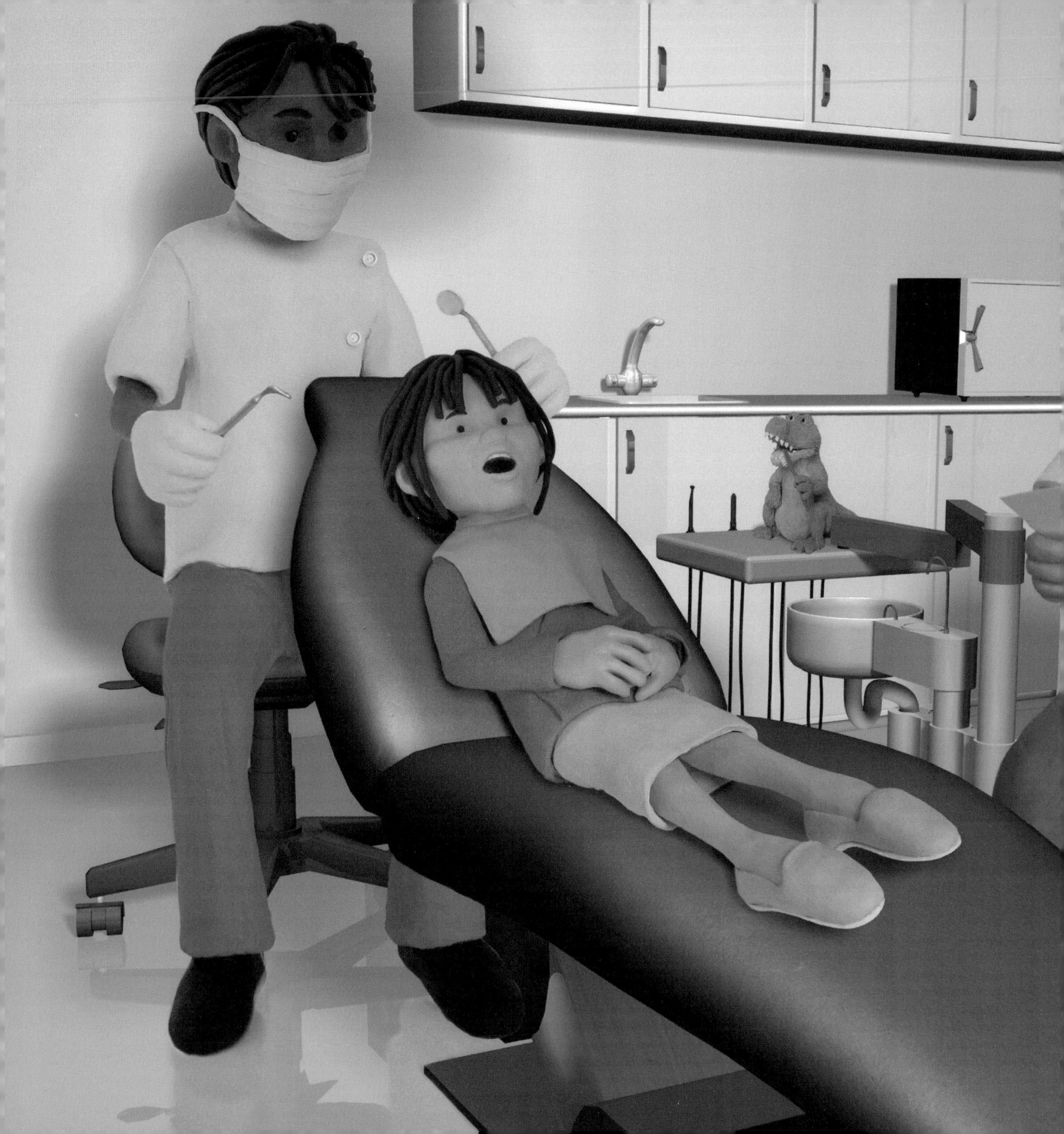

首先是检查雅思敏。牙医戴上手套和
口罩，他拿起一面小镜子检查她的牙齿。
他把椅子向后倾侧，然后检查她的牙齿，
护士则录下笔记。

It was Yasmin's turn first. The dentist put
on gloves and a mask. He picked up a small
mirror to examine her teeth.
He tilted the chair backwards and checked
her teeth while the nurse took notes.

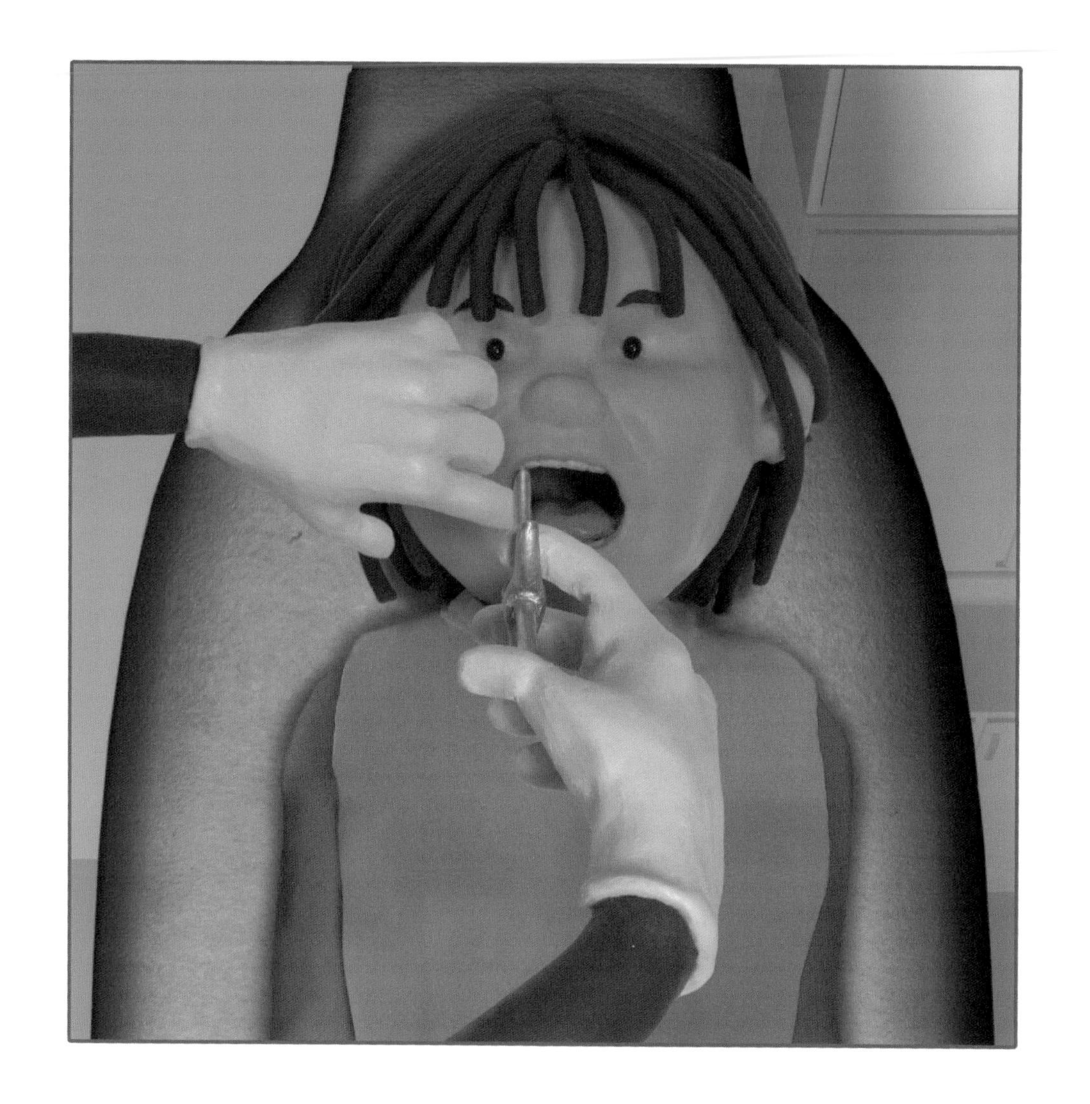

牙医发现雅思敏靠后的一只牙有一个齿窝。
「我们需要填补齿窝，」他说。「我会给你打针，
令你的齿龈麻木，不会觉得痛。」

The dentist noticed a hole in one of Yasmin's back teeth.
"We'll need to put a small filling in there," he said. "I'm going to give you an injection to numb your gum so that it won't hurt."

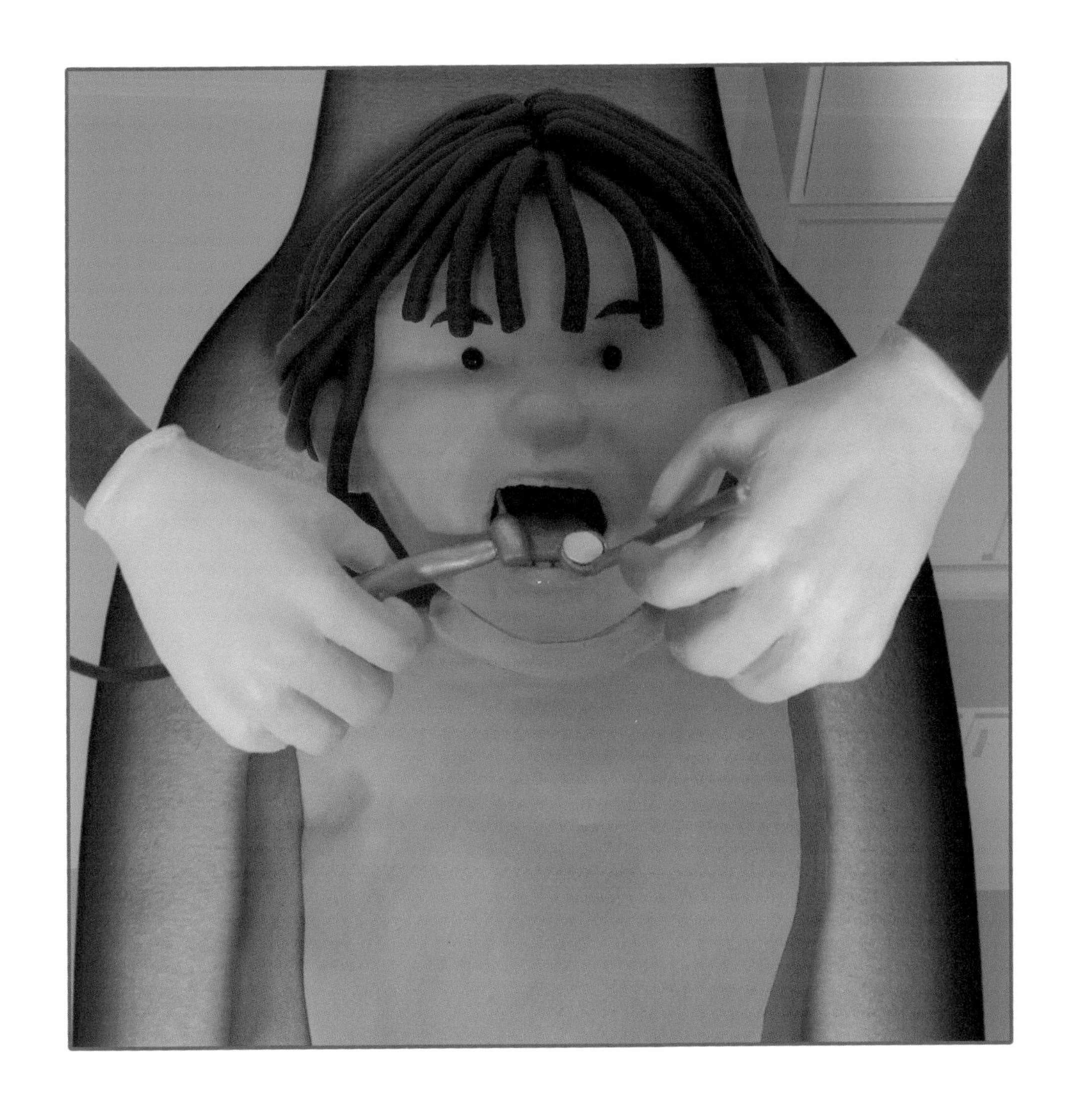

牙医跟着便用他的刮钻器清除牙齿的蛀坏部分。

Then the dentist removed the bad part of the tooth with his drill.

护士则用吸管保持雅思敏的口腔干爽，吸管咯咯地发出声响。

The nurse kept Yasmin's mouth dry using a suction tube. It made a noisy gurgling sound.

护士调制了一些特别的糊状混合物递给牙医。

The nurse mixed up a special paste and gave it to the dentist.

牙医小心地填补齿窝。「你看，做完了，」他说。
雅思敏漱一下口，然后吐进一个特别的瓷盘。

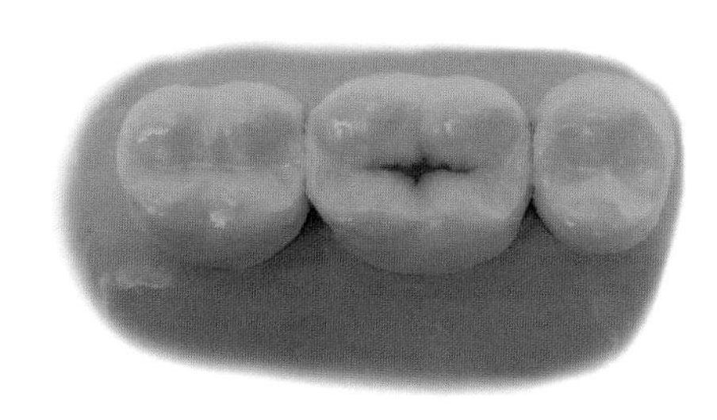

填补齿窝前 before filling

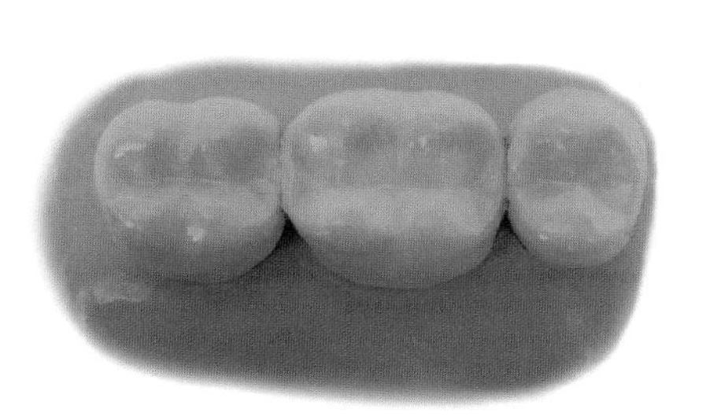

填补齿窝后 after filling

The dentist carefully filled the hole. "There you are, all done," he said.
Yasmin rinsed out her mouth and spat into a special basin.

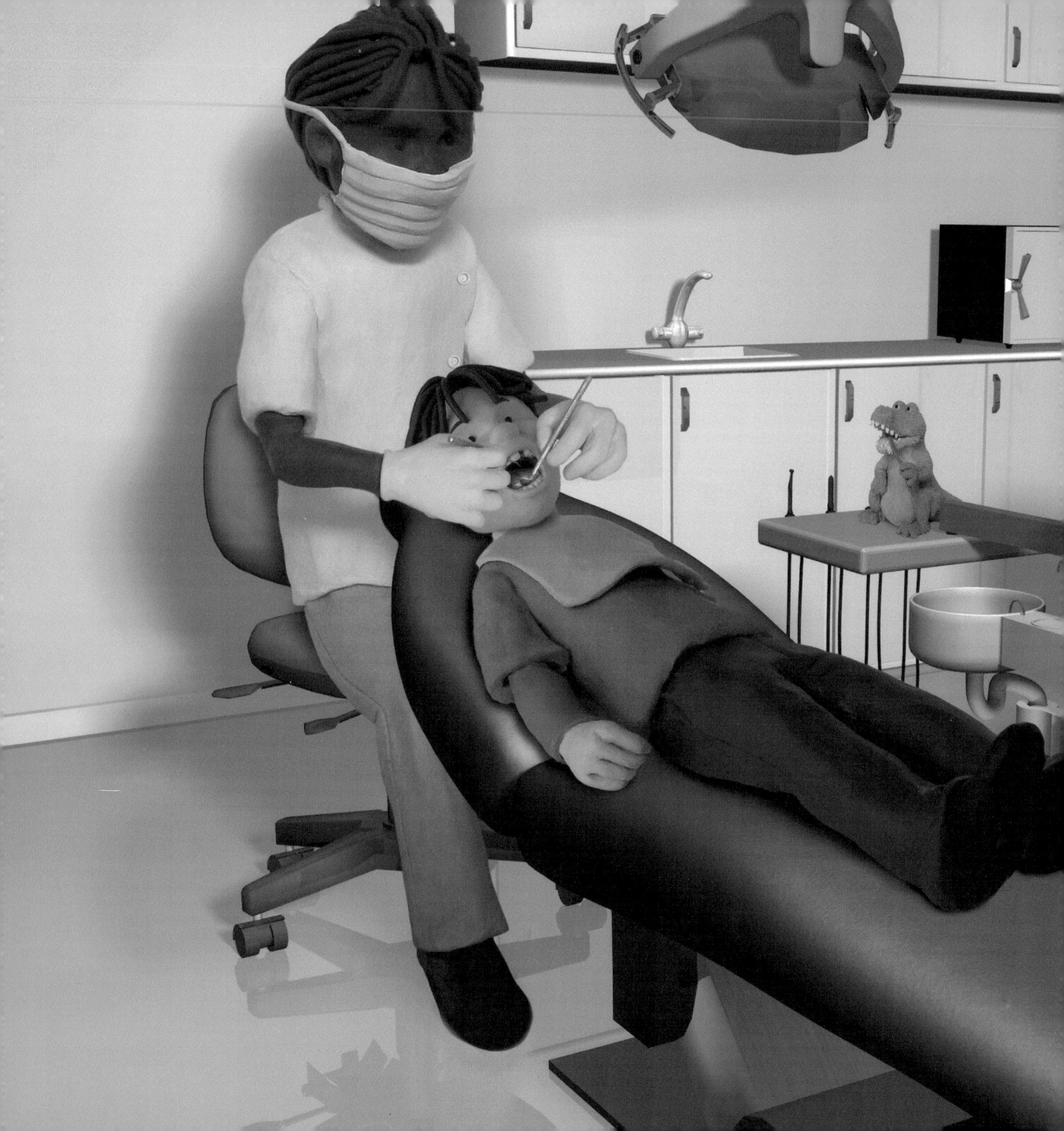

跟着便轮到撒希了。
牙医检查撒希的牙齿。
「很好，我看不到任何齿窝，」
他说，「但我看到你有新牙准备
长出来。」

It was Sahir's turn next.
The dentist examined Sahir's teeth.
"Good. I can't see any holes," he said.
"But I see you have new teeth coming
through."

「我们为你的牙齿造一个牙模，让我们可以较清楚地看到你的新牙如何成长出来，这是我们为一个小女孩造的牙模。」

"We will make a model of your teeth so we can see more clearly how your teeth are coming through. Here's a model we made for a young girl."

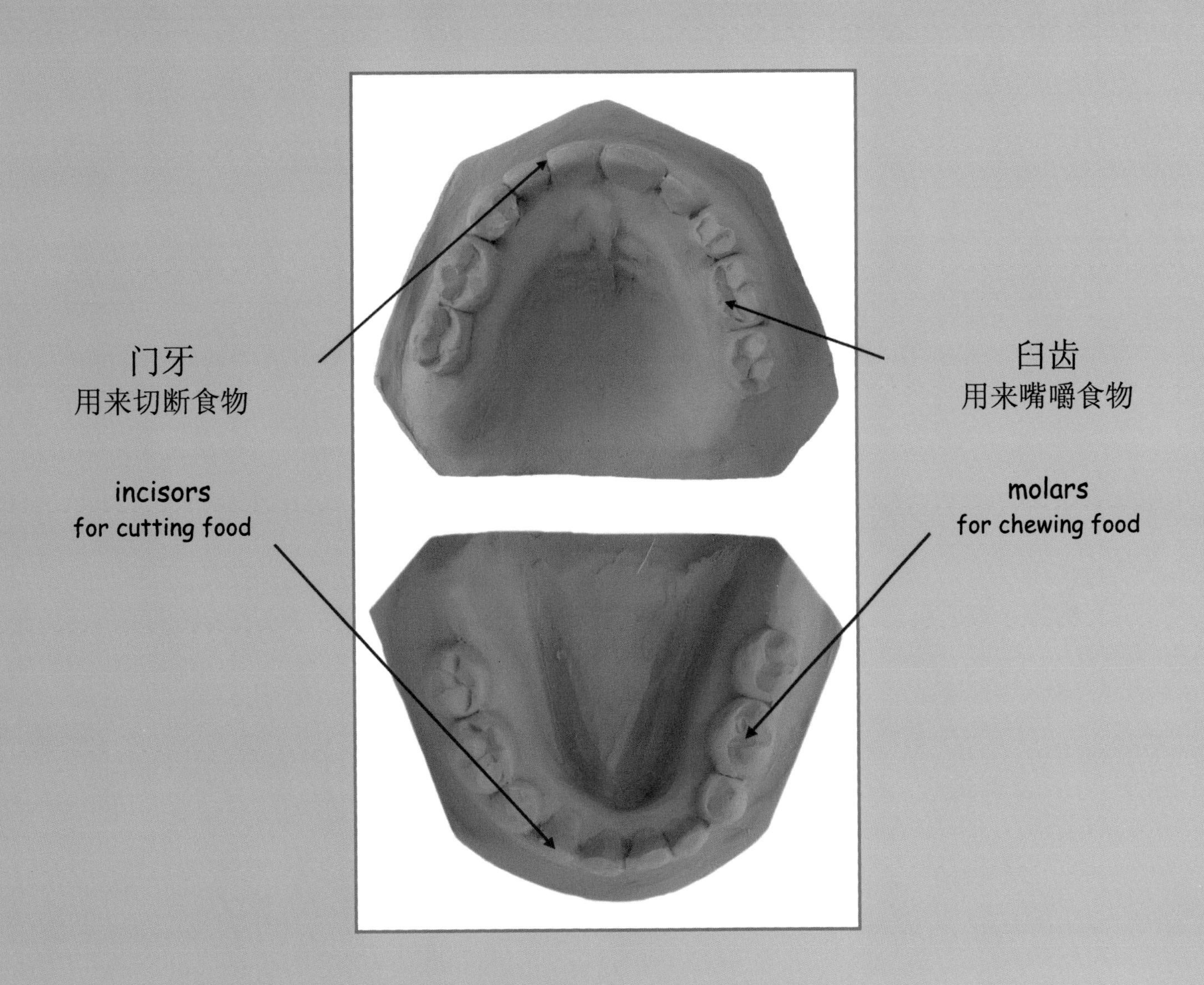

「张开嘴巴，」他说，跟着便将一个载满黏灰陶土的小盘套上撒希的上排牙齿，「现在紧紧咬著，让它凝固。」
接着他便将小盘拿开。

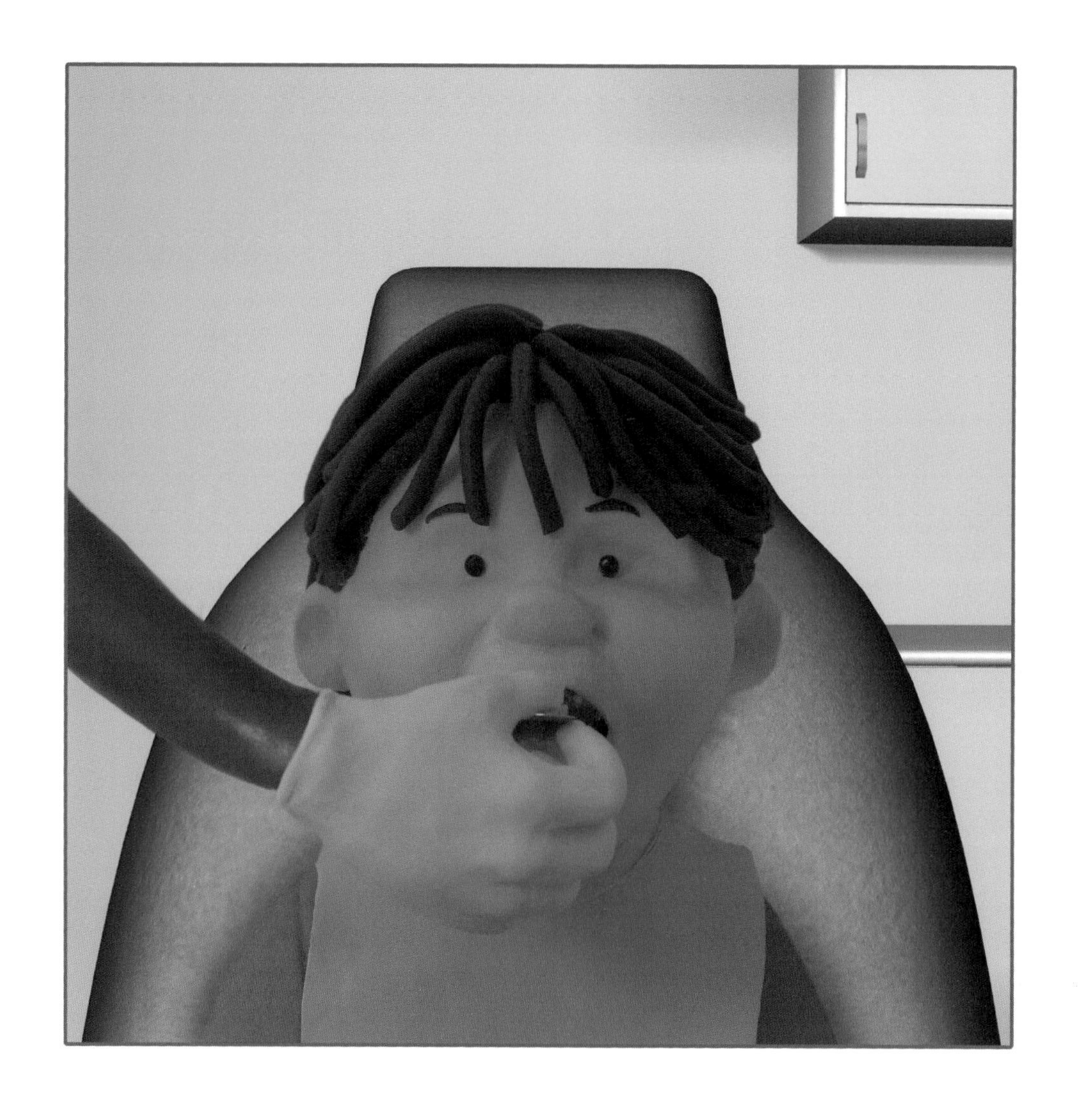

"Open wide," he said, and put a small tray filled with a gooey coloured dough over Sahir's top teeth. "Now bite down hard so that it sets." Then he removed it from Sahir's mouth.

牙医把造好的模型拿给撒希看。「我们将这个送到实验室去，他们会倒入石膏制成牙模，」牙医说。

The dentist showed Sahir the finished mould. "We send this to a laboratory where they pour in plaster to make the model," said the dentist.

雅思敏和撒希跟着便去见牙科卫生师。
「让我看看你们是怎样刷牙的，」她说道，
然后递了一枝牙刷给撒希。

Next Yasmin and Sahir went to see the hygienist.
"Let's see how you brush your teeth," she said, handing Sahir a toothbrush.

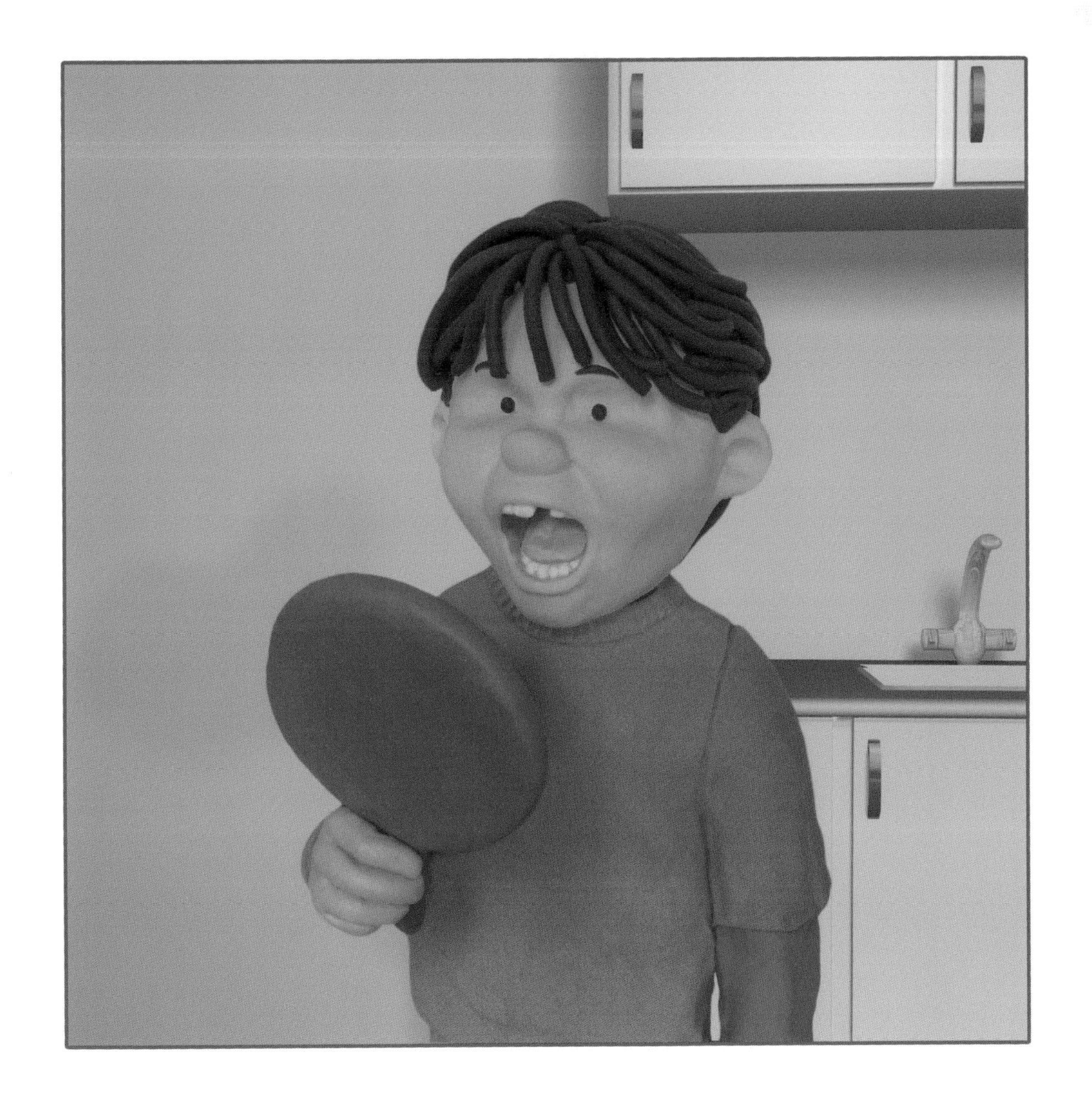

当撒希刷完牙后，卫生师便给他一颗粉红色的药丸，
让他放进口内嘴嚼。
「所有牙刷没有刷过的部分都会呈现出深粉红色。」

When Sahir had finished, the hygienist gave him a pink tablet to chew.
"All the places you missed with your toothbrush will show up as dark pink patches on your teeth."

她用一副巨大的牙齿向孩子们示范正确的刷牙方法。
「哗，它们好像恐龙的牙齿！」撒希屏息著说。

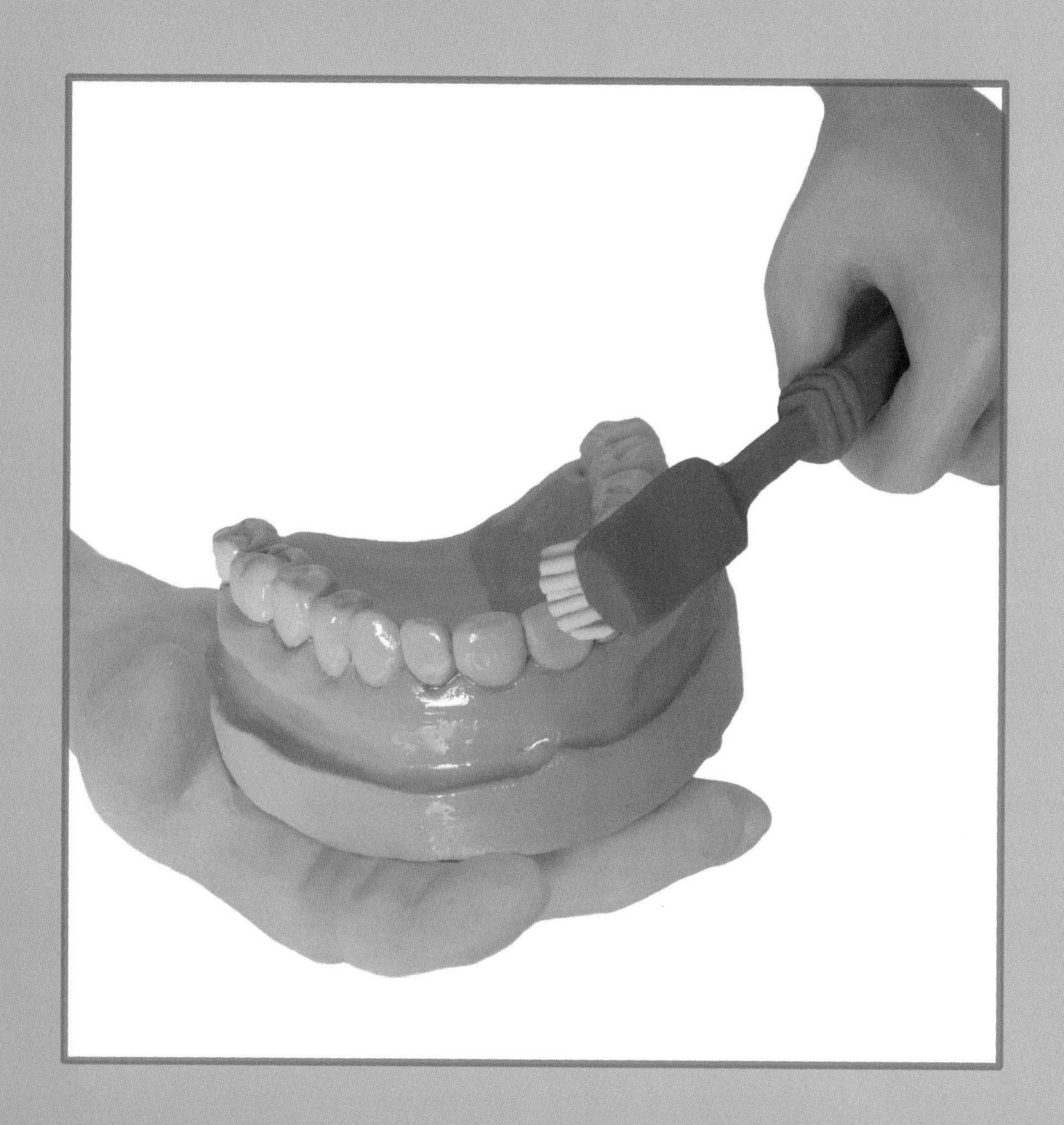

She showed the children the proper way to brush on a giant set of teeth.
"Wow, they're as big as dinosaurs' teeth," gasped Sahir.

「你需要向上向下地刷牙，在每一边都刷，
从前面刷到后面，」卫生师说。

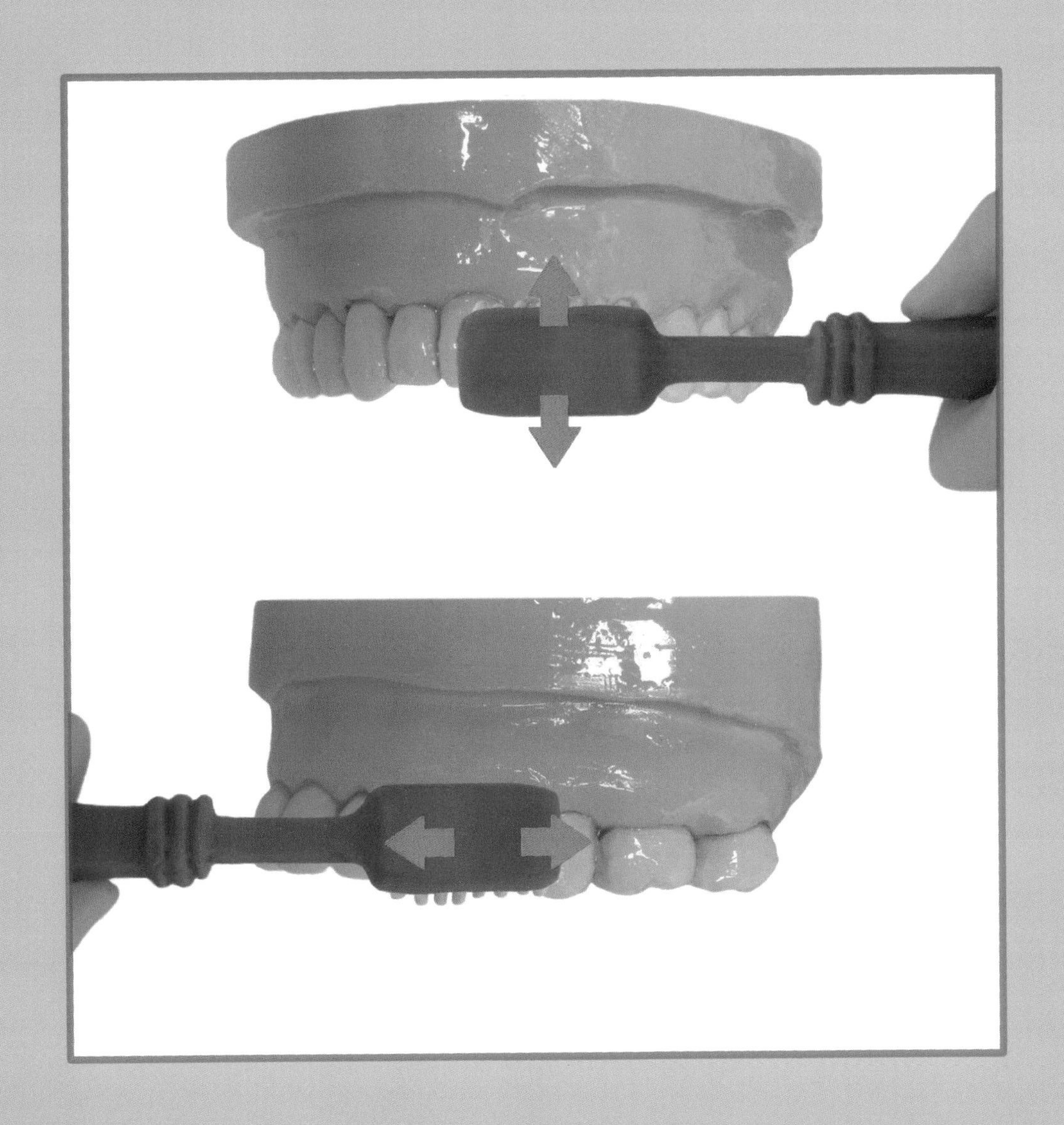

"You need to brush your teeth up and down. Then brush each side from front to back," the hygienist said.

她向孩子们出示一张海报。「这些细小的破坏份子叫做细菌，
它们侵蚀我们的牙齿，」卫生师说。「它们吞下糖份，制造酸物，
这样会在你的牙齿导致齿窝。」
「哦！」撒希说。

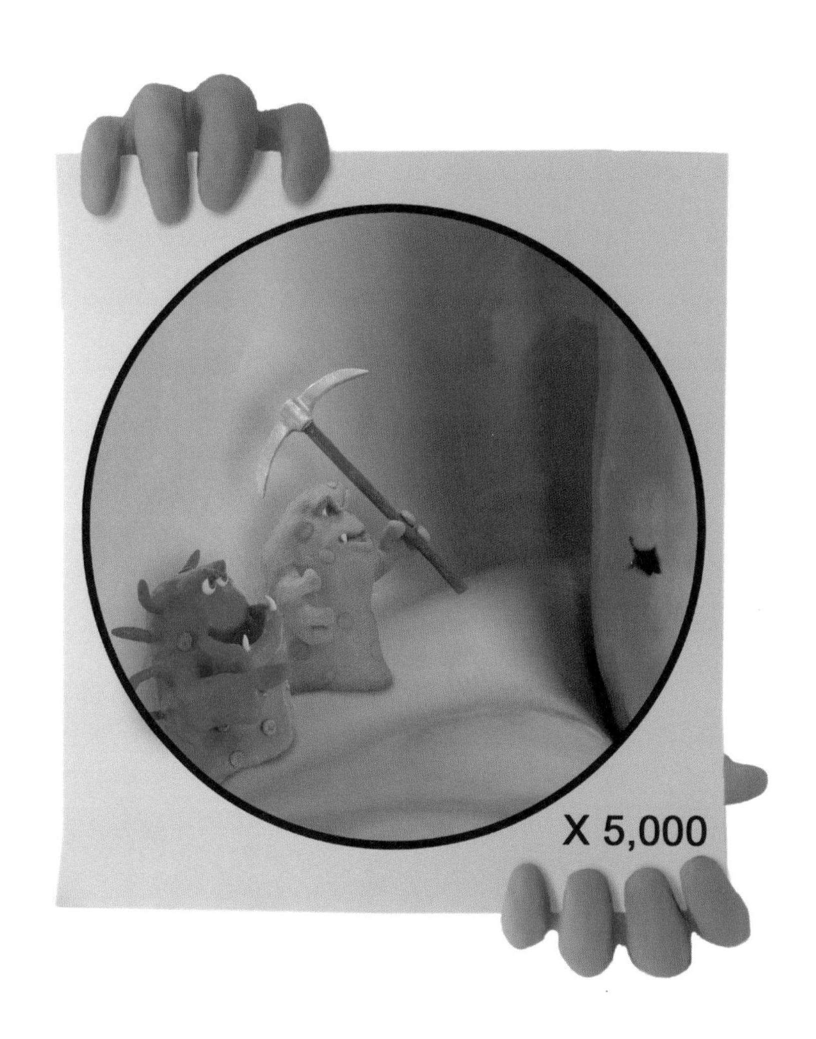

She showed the children a poster. “These tiny bad guys are called bacteria and attack our teeth,” said the hygienist. “They gobble up sugar and produce acid,” she said. “This can make holes in your teeth.”
“Yuck!” said Sahir.

「它们生存在牙齿上面一层称为牙垢的黏物，就是在你们的牙齿上呈现粉红色的黏状物，这些可恶的细菌最喜欢黏性甜食，」卫生师说。

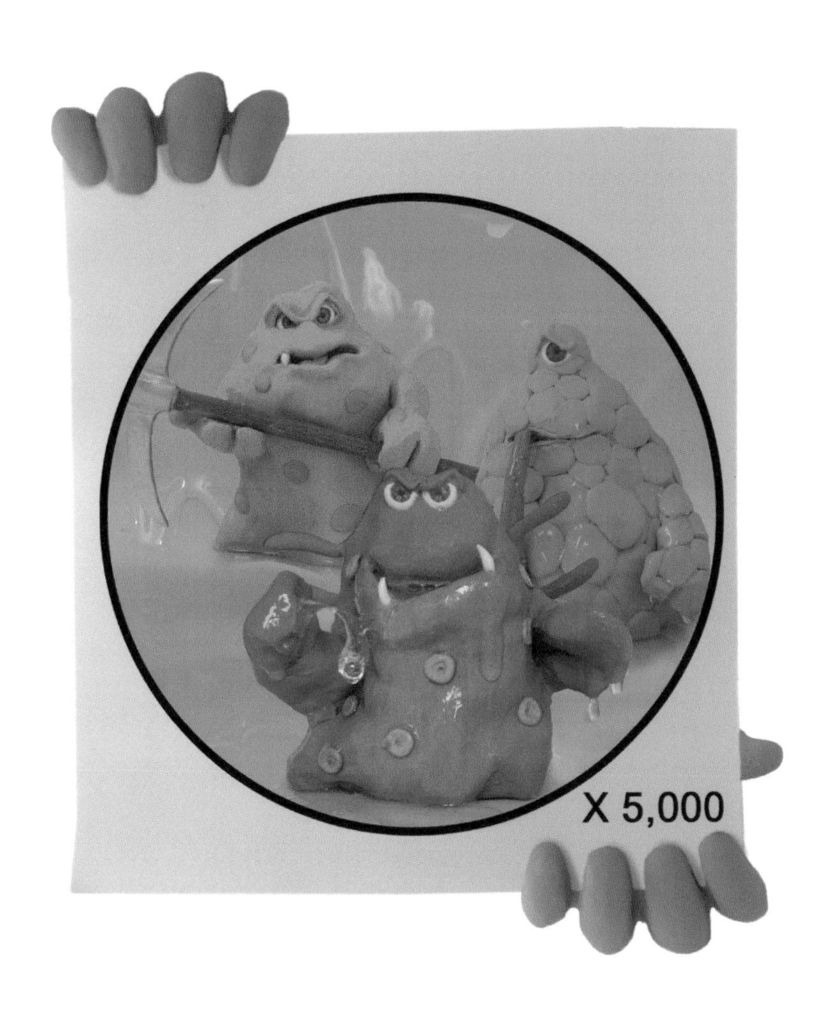

"They live in a sticky layer covering our teeth called plaque. This was shown up as pink on your teeth. The bad bacteria love sweet sticky foods," said the hygienist.

「所以最好少吃糖类食物，」卫生师说。

"So try and eat less sugar," said the hygienist.

她送孩子们一张标贴。「送这个给你们，因为你们是好孩子。如果你们像我向你们示范一样，小心地照料牙齿，你们的牙齿便会一直保持健康。」

She gave them both a sticker. "This is for being so good. And if you look after your teeth, like I've shown you, your teeth will always be healthy."

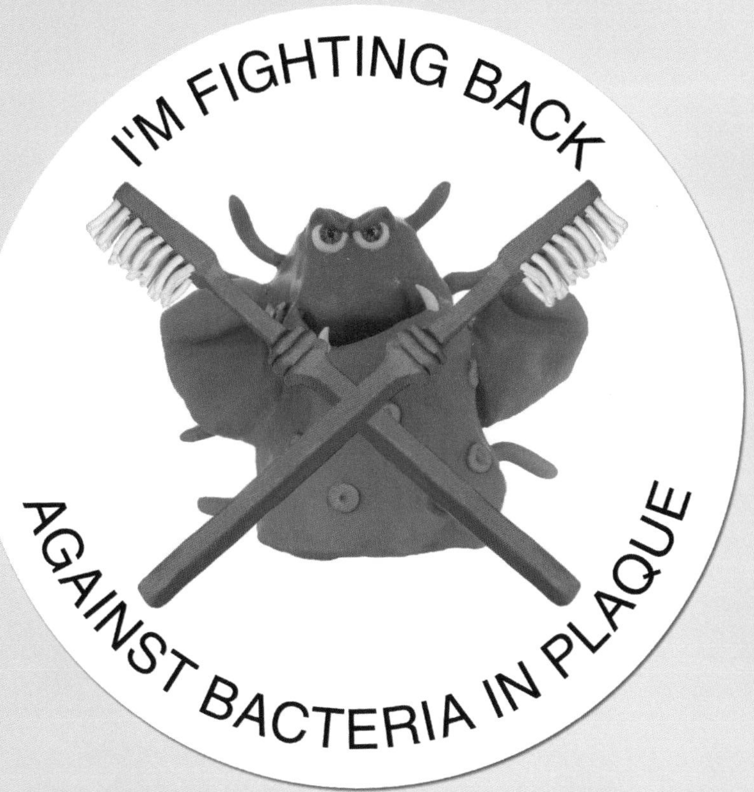

当他们离开诊所时，撒希向爸爸取回牙齿仙子给他的钱币。
「啊，」爸爸说，「你想买一大块巧克力。」
「不会呀！爸爸！」撒希说，「我想买一枝新的牙刷呢！」

As they left the surgery, Sahir asked Dad for the money the tooth fairy gave him.
"Ahh," said Dad. "You want to buy that big bar of chocolate."
"No way Dad!" said Sahir. "I want to buy... a brand new toothbrush!"

Sahir Goes to the Dentist

When Sahir loses a tooth, Dad decides to take him and Yasmin to the dentist. Yasmin needs a small filling and Sahir has a model made of his teeth. Then it's time to see the hygienist who shows them how to keep their teeth healthy. Chris Petty's friendly plasticine models will help to ease children's fears before they visit the dentist.

Sahir Goes to the Dentist is part of ***Mantra's First Experience*** Series.
Other titles in the Series:
Nita Goes to Hospital
Tom and Sofia Start School

I'M FIGHTING BACK AGAINST BACTERIA IN PLAQUE

Sahir Goes to the Dentist is available in 25 dual language editions: English with Albanian, Arabic, Bengali, Cantonese, Farsi, French, German, Greek, Gujarati, Hindi, Italian, Japanese, Kurdish, Mandarin, Panjabi, Polish, Portuguese, Russian, Somali, Spanish, Tagalog, Tamil, Turkish, Urdu or Vietnamese.